AZOR

By MAUDE CROWLEY

Pictures by HELEN SEWELL

HENRY Z. WALCK, INC.

PRINTED IN THE UNITED STATES OF AMERICA

For
David and Chrissie
and Erik

CHAPTER ONE

AZOR PEACH was six years old and he lived in a red house on Elm Street in Marblehead, Massachusetts. He was 47 inches tall, and he weighed 56 pounds, and he had six new teeth. So he was pretty big for his age.

Azor was in the First Grade at the Gerry School. He could read words like SOME-

So the morning after Mrs. Woodfin lost the silver earring that had belonged to her grandmother, he jumped down from his porch railing when he saw Azor leaving for school.

"That earring is behind the third right-hand fencepost on Dr. Snow's lawn," he said. "If you want to know."

"Thank you," said Azor.

And after school he walked down to Sapphire Lane and got it, and took it to Mrs. Woodfin's house. She wasn't home, but at suppertime she came to Azor's house and gave him a dollar.

"You're a good boy, Azor," she said, "to go hunting for my earring when you could have been playing with the other boys."

"I didn't go hunting for it," said Azor. "Larry Freeto told me where it was and I just went and got it."

Everybody was in the living-room, so they

all heard. His mother told him to stop telling stories to Mrs. Woodfin this very minute! His father said he was getting too old for this sort of thing and that it would have to stop. And his big brother Matthew told him not to be a baby *all* his life.

Azor only said "He really *did*," and went outside.

CHAPTER TWO

LARRY wasn't the only one who told him things. There was Ambrose Frost, too. Ambrose was Mr. Frost's horse. In the Winter he pulled the sidewalk snowplow, and in the Summer he pulled Mr. Frost's vegetable wagon. So he was around town a good part of the year. Ambrose knew everybody, and everybody knew Ambrose.

On Valentine Day there was a big snowstorm. As soon as it cleared, Azor went out to shovel snow off the front path. Across the street Chrissie Orne was shoveling too, and his little sister Pringle was trying to make a snowman. It wasn't very good because Pringle was so little.

Chrissie's path was shorter than Azor's, so when he had finished his own shoveling he came over to help Azor. Pringle came too, and started a new snowman in Azor's yard.

After a while Chrissie's mother sent him to the corner store for some baking chocolate, and while he was gone the postman came along and handed Azor a big envelope.

He opened it. It was a Valentine made like a boat. The part you sit in was made of pleated red tissue paper. When you pulled it out it made a deep rounded shape like a real rowboat. A girl with yellow curls was sitting in it smiling at him.

While he was looking at it Pringle came puffing and stumbling over through the deep snow. Her cheeks were as red as tomatoes and her eyes were bright blue. The sun made her hair look like shiny molasses taffy.

"Who's it from, Azor, who's it from?" she asked.

Azor turned it around and around. He looked at the back and at the front and under the red tissue paper. He even pulled off the stamp to look under that. But he found nothing.

"I don't know," he said. "It has no name on it."

So Pringle went back to her snowman.

Just then Ambrose came up the street pulling the plow. He had to stop in front of Azor's path while Mr. Frost lighted his pipe, and he stood watching Azor and the Valentine.

"I see you got one from Ella Snook," he said at last. Then Mr. Frost finished lighting his pipe and they went on up the street.

"Ambrose says it's from Ella Snook," Azor called to Pringle.

"Oh," she said, "maybe he saw her mail it."

CHAPTER THREE

So THE next day in school Azor knew why Ella Snook looked at him and giggled. When it was time to go home, he went over to her.

"Thank you for the Valentine," he said. "I didn't send you one because I didn't think you were going to send me one."

Ella shook her curls.

"How did you know it was from me?" she asked. "I didn't put my name on it. Anyway, I didn't send you any."

"Yes, you did," said Azor. "Ambrose told me."

David Crowley was sitting nearby pulling on his rubber boots, and he heard. So soon everybody was laughing and pointing at Azor.

"Mr. Frost's Ambrose!" they said.

"A HORSE!" they giggled.

"He says he TALKED to him!" they hooted.

And

"He's just like my little cousin Nora," laughed David.

"He never talks to *me*," Obed Frost said, "and he's *my* grandfather's *horse*!"

Then Miss Love, the teacher, said, "Children! Children! Quiet! Now form a line at the door—girls first."

So they had to stop. But when they got outside they began to tease Azor again, so he said "Goodbye" and started across the schoolyard.

On the sidewalk by the gate he met Ambrose with the plow. Ambrose looked over his shoulder as he passed and said, "If they knew more they'd say less."

And Azor started to whistle.

But that day Azor promised himself that hereafter he would mind his own business and keep his mouth shut.

"Now I see where my big mouth gets me," he said.

He only broke his promise once.

CHAPTER FOUR

AFTER that there were four snowstorms, one right after the other, and Azor coasted every day on Cowell Street. The police came and roped it off so no cars could come on it.

He took out his skis, too. Of course it was hard at first. He fell down 14 times the first day and 11 times the second day. But the seventh day he only fell down two times, and that was because his mother had put too much wax on his skis and they were too slippery.

He saw Ambrose every time there was a new storm, but he was too busy plowing to even notice Azor. Once, though, Ambrose saw the skis cross themselves in back of Azor, and he said, "Watch the left rear."

And Azor did. He lifted his left-foot ski off his right-foot ski and didn't fall after all.

All Winter and Spring Azor kept the promise he had made himself. Larry Freeto and Ambrose told him many interesting things, but he kept them all to himself.

He knew Matthew had signed his own Spring report card, but he kept quiet. He knew it was going to snow on Easter, but he said nothing when he saw his mother pressing her new Spring suit Good Friday.

When Miss Love lost her gold watch he knew where it was but he let her find it herself. And in May he knew that school would be closed for a whole week because of measles, but he kept his mouth shut.

Then school was over for the year, and the swimming started. Every day he went down Orne Street to Gashouse Beach. The sun was hot and the water was cold and the seagulls squawked over the water. He was sandy all the time. There was even sand in his bed at night, where it ran out from between his toes.

Sometimes Azor and Chrissie went way down to Oliver's Beach near Peach's Point, when the tide was out. They walked all over the flats in the cold clear water and watched the small crabs scrambling around on the bottom.

Once they saw a huge black lobster come crawling slowly up behind a big crab. They stayed long enough to see the fight start, but then the claws came too close to their toes, and they swam away—fast.

CHAPTER FIVE

AZOR very nearly broke his promise in August.

Early one morning he saw his brother, Matthew, and Chrissie's brother, Jimmer, starting down toward Orne Street. He knew right away where they were going, because they were carrying nets on long poles.

Matthew and Jimmer were going up to Black Joe's Pond to catch turtles to sell for 25 cents apiece to the children in town. That was before the lady who owned the pond found out what they were doing. When she did, she wouldn't let them come any more. She said it was cruel.

Azor had always wanted to go along with them, because if he could catch even one turtle

himself, he would have 25 whole cents, and he could go down to the store on the Town Wharf and for once in his life eat *enough* potato chips. But Matthew had always said he was too little— that he would only talk and scare the turtles away. So he was very much surprised when his brother called to him, "Hey, Azor! You can come along this time if you want to, because we need someone to watch the box so they won't get away. We're going to stay all day and catch millions! But remember — no talking! Hear?"

Azor would much rather have brought a net and tried to catch some himself, but it was better to go along and not catch any, than not to go at all. So he ran back into the kitchen and got a piece of chocolate cake and a bottle of root beer from the icebox. Then he raced after Matthew and Jimmer, and caught up with them at the foot of Gingerbread Lane.

When they got to Black Joe's they dug a hole at the edge of the pond where the water was very shallow, and put their bottles of root beer in it to keep cool. Matthew and Jimmer hauled a big box from behind the old red house that had once been Black Joe's Tavern and put it in the grass under a tree.

They left Azor beside it with the lunches, and told him not to make a sound. Then they went down to the edge of the water with their nets. They threw some bread crumbs out and waited for the turtles to come.

CHAPTER SIX

WHILE AZOR sat and watched them he thought of what his father had told him about Black Joe and the pond.

He said that the bottom of the pond was probably paved with pennies! Hundreds of years ago, the town people used to come up to Black Joe's Tavern on holidays. They ate buns and drank root beer, and at night the women danced and the men pitched pennies. Sometimes, when they weren't winning the game, they would get angry and toss their pennies right into the water.

Pretty soon Matthew and Jimmer began to bring turtles and put them into the box. By lunchtime they had seven. While they all drank their root beer and ate their cake Azor listened to them talking.

"Jingoes!" said Matthew. "You know how much money that is? That's one dollar and seventy-five cents! That's how much! And we have the whole afternoon to go!"

"If we get seven more this afternoon," Jimmer said, "it will be more than July Doliber and his whole gang ever got in one day!"

"It won't be, if you stay here all afternoon talking," said Azor.

So they went down to the water again. After a while they brought two more turtles, and then there was a long time when they didn't bring any. Azor lay on his stomach looking into the box.

There was a big one in there and a couple of medium ones, but the rest were tiny ones born that very Spring. Some of them had their heads and paws drawn into their shells and their pointed little tails wrapped across their bottoms. The ones who didn't, crawled around and looked up at Azor as if they weren't afraid, or even surprised, that they had been caught.

Azor wondered how it was to be a turtle, and the very second he was wondering that, the biggest turtle blinked his eyes slowly and looked up at him.

"Make it worth your while if you tip the box," he said. "Same time, same place, tomorrow."

So Azor turned over the box and watched them crawl over the grass and plop back into the pond. He was glad the littlest ones were going back to their mothers.

But when the last one had slid down into the water he suddenly thought of Matthew and Jimmer down by the pond, and he started to feel quite queer. He thought it was probably time to go home. So he did.

CHAPTER SEVEN

Azor got tired very fast that night, because every place he went in the house Matthew seemed to be there ahead of him with his jaw stuck way out and shaking his fist.

Finally his mother said, "What's the matter with you children tonight?"

So Azor told her, and that made Matthew even madder than he was before. The second Azor saw his brother starting to get madder, he remembered that his mother didn't like Matthew to sell turtles, but by then he was in the middle of the story and he had to finish it. The only thing he didn't tell was why he tipped the box.

After that he went up to bed. While he was

getting undressed he heard his mother being
angry at Matthew, and he thought it had been
a quite angry day, and went to sleep.

35

The next day he only had time to get to the pond and sit down under the tree when the big turtle came crawling up out of the water.

He had something in his mouth that looked like an old penny, only much bigger—almost as big as a half-dollar. He dropped it in the grass in front of Azor. It was all wet and gunky, and Azor didn't even want to touch it, but he picked it up and put it in his pocket.

"Thank you very much," he said.

Then the turtle went away and Azor went back home.

After supper he was in the kitchen polishing the penny so it would look better, and not

smell so awful, when his father came in. He watched Azor for a minute, and then he asked him where the penny came from.

That was the moment when Azor nearly broke the vow he had made after Valentine Day, because he opened his mouth to say, "The turtle gave it to me for tipping the box." But he caught himself just in time. It wasn't until September that he really broke the promise—but then he *had* to.

"I got it up by Black Joe's Pond," he told his father.

His father picked up the penny and looked at it.

"Hmh!" he said. "I'm going to take this over to Lot Snow and see what *he* thinks. I'll be right back."

And he was gone. Mr. Snow was the man who last year gave 25 cents to everyone who brought him an Indian-head penny.

Azor was brushing his teeth for bed when his father came back and called him in a loud voice—not an angry-loud voice, but a pleased-loud voice.

"Azor! Come on down here!"

When he got downstairs everybody was in the living-room, and Matthew's mouth was quite wide open, but he wasn't saying anything. He was just staring at a pile of money on the table.

"Well, Azor," his father said. "You're a rich man. That old penny of yours was a 1793 Cent—one of the first coins we ever made in this country! Lot Snow bought it for FORTY-SEVEN DOLLARS! Pick it up, son, it's all yours."

And Azor picked it up. Except for potato chip money it went into the bank with the money Azor was saving for a sailboat when he got to be twelve.

CHAPTER EIGHT

THE NEXT day Matthew was very pleasant. For a whole week Azor had to take him and Jimmer Orne up to Black Joe's to show them the exact spot where he had found the penny. Every time, he showed them just where the turtle had dropped it, but he never once mentioned the turtle. The boys soon got tired of hunting, and after Labor Day school began again.

One evening in September they were having supper when Jimmer came flying in, all excited.

"My mother can't find Pringle!" he said. "And it's getting night, so my father is going out to look for her in the car, and I'm going too. Can Matthew and his father come?"

Azor's father got up from the table without finishing his supper, and Azor's mother said Matthew could go, too. They took their flashlights in case it got dark before they found Pringle. After they had gone, Azor and his mother went across the street to stay with Mrs. Orne.

Mrs. Orne was nearly always laughing and whistling, but tonight she looked very, very worried. She said she had looked everywhere and asked everyone, but no one had seen Pringle. There was nothing for her to do but sit and wait, in case Pringle came home by herself. So his mother sat down with her and Azor went out with Chrissie to swing on the swings in the yard.

When it was almost dark his father and Mr. Orne came home and ran up the steps. Azor heard them talking in the house.

Mr. Orne said that if Pringle hadn't been

found by eight o'clock, the policemen and firemen and Boy Scouts were going to be called out. His father said it was a warm night and for Mrs. Orne to try not to worry too much. Then they ran down the steps again and got into the car and drove off.

After a while Azor and Chrissie went down to Washington Street and stood outside the Town Hall. They saw a lot of policemen come out of the police station and get into cars. Then three cars with firemen in went by, and they noticed that there were a lot of Boy Scouts walking around with flashlights in their belts.

Matthew and Jimmer were with the Boy Scouts—they were both Cubs. They said the Scouts were going to look in every inch of the woods and fields around Black Joe's Pond. The fathers were going to look in all the other places Pringle had ever been or could possibly have got lost in. And the policemen and firemen

were going to look in the pastures between Marblehead and Salem.

Everybody went, and there was no one left in the street, so Azor and Chrissie went home and their mothers made them go to bed because it was after nine o'clock.

CHAPTER NINE

PRINGLE was not found that night. The next day there was no school, and Chrissie was down at his grandmother's house on Front Street, so Azor didn't have much to do.

After lunch he went down to Gashouse to get some of the little pink crabshells you always see down there. He got a whole pocketful, and then he waded out and climbed into an old rowboat that was tied to a stake near the shore.

For a long time he sat there thinking about Pringle and her taffy hair, and watching the seagulls. They were flying around above him making the noises they make, and once in a while one of them would dive and pick a shining little fish out of the water with its beak.

The sun was starting to sink and the breeze was getting cold, and Azor had just stood up to go home for supper when one of the gulls swooped very near his head and said, "Just came by Peach's Point. She's out there asleep under the raft on the Baileys' beach — been playing house for two days."

"Oh," Azor said. Then he climbed out of the boat and waded back to shore.

Now Azor knew he would have to break his promise at last. For Pringle. If only they didn't ask him how he knew, he might still get out of mentioning the seagull.

When he got home his mother was out, so he went over to Chrissie's house. Police Chief Martin was there, and his father, and Mr. Orne and some other men. Mrs. Orne looked as if she had been crying.

There was a whole lot of talk about where everybody had been, and Mr. Martin said there wasn't one inch of Marblehead that hadn't been looked in, or one person who hadn't been asked.

"Except me," said Azor. "And *I* know where she *is*."

Everybody looked at him with their mouths open and their eyes bugged out. Then they all rushed at him.

"WHERE?" they shouted.

"She's asleep under the raft on the Baileys' beach."

Then Mrs. Orne *really* started to cry, and his mother said:

"Why, why, WHY didn't you tell us BEFORE?"

"Because I only just found it out," said Azor.

Then Police Chief Martin put his hand on Azor's shoulder and told him this was a very, very serious time. He said the second night was

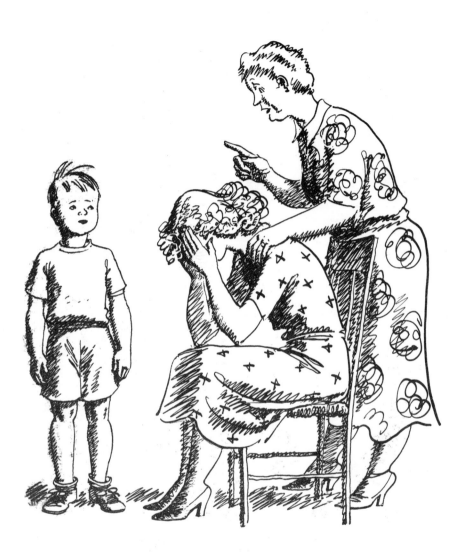

coming and that not a single minute could be
wasted in useless hunting.

"It isn't useless hunting," Azor said. "She's there all right."

"But we've been to Peach's Point already, Azor, and she *wasn't* there," said Mr. Martin. "What makes you so sure she is?"

Then Azor knew it was no use. He told.

When they heard about the seagull, his father and mother were *very* angry. Mrs. Orne sank back into her chair and covered her face with her hands. And Chief Martin was furious. But at last he said, "Well, we haven't looked *under* the rafts, at that—come on!"

And the men went out.

CHAPTER TEN

NOBODY said anything more to Azor, so he and Chrissie went out into the yard and skinned the cat on a bar. After they had each done it a few times Chrissie let go of the bar too soon and landed on his head in the grass. He had just put his hand up to his head to rub it when there was the sound of cars outside and lots of people talking and laughing.

Then Mrs. Orne and Azor's mother came running out of the door so fast they nearly knocked each other over, and it took them a second to get staightened out.

They saw Mr. Orne coming up the walk with Pringle in his arms, and Pringle was howling "Mummy!" but she was all right. Chief

Martin and Azor's father came after him, and
in the street behind them Azor could see policemen and firemen and Boy Scouts, and there
was a lot of shouting.

After Mr. Orne had given Pringle to her
mother, he walked to the gate and said very

loud, so everyone in the yard and the street
could hear, "I want you all to know that it was

Azor Peach who *really* found Pringle."

Everybody looked at everybody else and then someone started to shout "Three cheers for Azor!" They kept on shouting it, and Azor could see Matthew out there jumping up and down and shouting louder than anyone.

When they had stopped a little, Chief Martin went to the gate. The sun was just going down, and the rays shone full on the star on his cap. He held up his hand and then he said, "And *I* want you to know that if Azor Peach says animals tell him things, you can bet your bottom dollar they do!"

Chief Martin looked very stern and everybody was very, very quiet. Then Azor's father took hold of Azor's hand and they both went over and stood beside Chief Martin.

"Yes," his father said in a loud voice. "They REALLY DO."

So that was that.